FHM

Get **more** out of libraries

Please return or renew this item by the last date shown.

You can renew online at www.hants.gov.uk/library

Or by phoning 0300 555 1387

Hampshire
County Council

ReadZone Books Limited
www.ReadZoneBooks.com

© in this edition 2015 ReadZone Books Limited

This print edition published in cooperation with Fiction Express, who first published this title in weekly instalments as an interactive e-book.

FICTI⬤N EXPRESS

Fiction Express
First Floor Office, 2 College Street,
Ludlow, Shropshire SY8 1AN
www.fictionexpress.co.uk

Find out more about Fiction Express on pages 86–87.

Design: Laura Durman & Keith Williams
Cover Image: Shutterstock Images

© in the text 2015 Alex Woolf
The moral right of the author has been asserted.

ISBN 978-1-78322-550-7

Printed in Malta by Melita Press.

MIND
SWAP

Alex Woolf

What do other readers think?

Here are some comments left on the Fiction Express blog about this book:

"We both really enjoyed the book Mind Swap…
Out of 10 we would give it 11.5!!"
Mia and Jorja, Shropshire

*"This book was amazing. I loved the storyline and
once I started reading I couldn't put it down."*
Emily Alderson, Northampton

"I loved Mind Swap. *I loved how there were
TWO real Simon Archers. It was funny.
I hope I see another book by [Alex Woolf] soon!!!"*
Madi Mills, Sandye Place Academy

"This book was EPIC!!!"
Fran and Oliver, Shrewsbury

*"*Mind Swap *was one of the best books I have ever read."*
Izzy, Bedfordshire

Contents

Chapter 1

The Class Joker

It's half past two. Still an hour to go before the end of school! How will I survive? Grimes the geography teacher is droning on about oxbow lakes – who cares? Kids are nodding off in their seats. Grimes has to be the dullest person on this planet. Dull voice, dull hair, dull clothes. The only thing interesting about him is his left arm – or lack of it. Half of it is missing. His jacket sleeve is empty and flat below the elbow. He never talks about that, and really hates it when we ask him about it.

But sometimes, when I'm *this* bored, I can't help myself. I just have to shake things up.

"Sir?" I suddenly shout. "Tell us how you lost your arm."

Grimes spins around from the whiteboard, pen in hand. He gives me a fierce, bulge-eyed stare. "I've told you before, Simon Archer. Do *not* disrupt this class with inappropriate questions!"

"I just want to know, sir," I persist, "because I never knew it could be that dangerous – being a geography teacher, I mean. What's the worst that can happen? A paper cut from a map?" I can hear the sniggers starting up around me, and I know I have to carry on. I can't help it – they expect it of me. "Tell us what happened, sir. Did a field trip go wrong? Is that why they won't let you go on field trips any more? Wouldn't be much good now anyway, would you? Not with just one arm!"

By now a few kids are openly laughing. Most of the rest are staring hard at their desks, looking as if they'd rather be somewhere else. Wimps! They should be grateful I've saved them all from death by boredom.

Grimes turns purple. "How dare you be so rude! One more word out of you, boy, and you're in detention! You hear?"

I chortle to myself, amused to see him so flustered. He turns back to the board. "Oxbow l-lakes," he stammers, "are created when a-a river… forms a meander due to the, um, erosion of the bank by… by…"

"By oxen, sir?" I suggest.

"I'm warning you, Archer!" he hisses.

"It's those greedy bankers, ain't it?" says my mate Tom Hazlitt, sniggering. "They've eroded all the banks."

The class collapses with laughter. Grimes looks as if he's ready to explode.

"Hydraulic action, abrasion and corrosion, sir?" says Dylan Fox, the class swot.

"Yes, that's right," Grimes smiles gratefully at him. "Thank you, Dylan."

Grrrr!!! Just as Grimes was about to throw a wobbly. That kid does not deserve to live!!!

"We nearly had him," Tom whispers to me.

"Foxy will pay for that!" I grimace.

Grimes is now back in boring lecture mode, and I'm still feeling restless. But then I see something that brings a smile back to my face. Clare Philpott, the girl on my right, has got her bag on her lap and is secretly scoffing a sandwich she's got hidden in it. She's stuffing little bits into her gob when she thinks no one's looking. It's not the first time I've caught her doing that.

"Alright greedy guts!" I call loudly to her. "Lunch wasn't enough for you then, hey, Philpott? Do you ever *stop* eating?"

Everyone turns in time to see Clare with her mouth full, crumbs all over her face. She's blushing like a beetroot as she wipes her cheeks and tries to swallow it all down.

"Right, that's it!" declares Grimes. "Detention for you, Archer. Tomorrow after school."

I just lean back and bask in the laughter of my classmates. An hour's detention is well worth it for the kick I get out of being class joker, and humiliating idiots like Grimes and Clare Philpott!

After class, there's some business to be settled with little Dylan Fox. My mate Dev joins Tom and me as we corner him by the lockers. He looks up at us with big frightened eyes, then tries to make a break for it, squeezing between me and Dev. But we close ranks, shoving him back against a locker. He's clutching some mechanical thing close to his chest. I snatch it off him and take a closer look. It seems to be the hand of a robot.

"Trying to build Terminator, are you?" I grin, dangling it in front of him mockingly. "Think Arnie can protect you from us?"

"Give it back!" he says, making a grab for it.

I whisk it clear.

"I'm late for computer club," he whimpers. "Please let me go."

"Oh no, you're late for computer club," I whine, mimicking his wimpy tone. "Well, you'd better run then, hadn't you!" I stand aside. "Be my guest."

He looks at me uncertainly. "Can I have my invention back?" he asks.

"What, *this*?" I love his look of fear and desperation as I wave the hand about.

He makes another grab for it, but I lob it to Dev, who chucks it to Tom. Dylan is piggy in the middle, making frantic lunges for his precious robo-hand as we pass it gleefully between us. As we're all so much bigger than him, it's easy to keep it out of his reach. When Tom tosses it to me, I pretend to fumble it.

"Whoops!" I say as it falls to the floor. "I'm all fingers and thumbs today!"

Sadly, it doesn't break.

Dylan immediately dives, but before he can reach it, my foot comes down hard on the metal mitt. There's a satisfying crunch of breaking cogs, rivets and springs.

The kid stares forlornly at the mess on the floor.

I shove my forefinger in his face. "Maybe that'll teach you not to spoil our fun with

Grimes. Next time you want to play teacher's pet, Foxy, button your lip."

Our point made, we leave him there, picking up the pieces of his mangled project.

"Looks like he's going to need a 'hand' with that!" I joke and we all laugh.

* * *

That evening, Mum burns the pizza… again!

"You expect me to eat that?" I say, pushing the plate aside.

"I'm sorry, love. I lost track of the time," she says, driving the iron across one of my white school shirts.

A bubble of anger rises in my chest. I have to punish her. "You're *useless*!" I scream at her. "You can't cook! You can't do anything! No wonder Dad walked out on you!"

That did it. Any mention of Dad always brings on the tears. Her lips start shaking. She slams the iron down on the metal holder. "I'm not useless," she whispers fiercely, wiping her eye. "I'm trying. I'm trying my *best*. But you don't make it easy, Simon. I never get any help from you."

"Don't blame me for your failures," I sneer at her. "Tom's mum never burns pizza. In fact, she never *cooks* pizza. He gets decent grub 'round his house – Jamie-Oliver-type stuff, you know."

Scored a bullseye with that one. Hit her where it hurts – her pride! She's really blubbing now.

Satisfied, I help myself to a bag of crisps and head for my room, smirking. I'm so hard!

Chapter 2

Transformed!

The next morning, I wake up feeling strange. I had an odd night. Weird dreams. Can't remember them now. But never mind. Another day awaits. More fun and games! I do like school. I like the respect I get there. I never have to fight for a seat on the bus. Some kid will always give up his for me… wouldn't dare not to! And when I get hungry, someone will offer me his packed lunch… whether he wants to or not! And there's no worries about getting caught – most of the teachers are too scared to tell me off. Heh heh! Oh yes, school is good!

I yawn, get out of bed and reach for my dressing gown hanging up behind the door. But for some reason, it's not there.

That's odd. Where's my dressing gown?

For that matter, where's my door?

I look around, and that's when I get a real shock. This isn't my room. The furniture's all different. And my Top Gear poster's gone, replaced by the Periodic Table of Elements. What's going on? Did someone move me to a different house during the night?

I run out of the room and down the stairs. I almost carry on running right out of the house, until I realize I'm still in my pyjamas…

Pyjamas?

I normally sleep in boxers and a t-shirt!

A woman I've never seen before comes into the entrance hall. She's dressed in a smart business suit. "Ah, there you are, Dylan," she says. "You're late, and I have to leave for work soon! Hurry up and get your breakfast."

I look behind me to see who she's talking to, but there's no one there but me.

"There's been a mistake," I tell her. "I'm not Dylan."

"Of course you are, dear. Who else would you be?"

I'm starting to get angry. "Are you blind or something, lady? Do I look like Dylan to you?"

She glares at me. "I can't say I care very much for that tone of voice, young man. Now stop all this nonsense and come and eat."

I realize then that she must be deluded – a mad, lonely woman who's kidnapped me, then convinced herself that I'm her son. I'll have to handle this carefully. She might be dangerous.

"Look at me," I tell her, turning around to face the hallway mirror. "Does this look like…"

And then I stop.

There in the mirror, staring back at me in his spotless, stripy pyjamas, is Dylan Fox. The same Dylan Fox whose robot hand I broke yesterday. The same Dylan Fox I've been teasing and taunting and harassing pretty much every day since he started at our school.

Somehow I've… *turned into… into Foxy!!!*

Like a zombie, I let Mrs Fox lead me into the kitchen. I'm in such a daze, I don't even notice at first that there's no breakfast waiting there for me. In the end, sheer hunger forces me to pour myself some cereal. I eat it without tasting a thing.

Dylan Fox? This is a total nightmare! If I had to turn into someone else, why couldn't it have been someone cool like James Bond or something, rather than the nerdiest boy in school.

Mr Fox is also there at the table, though I don't see or hear much of him as he spends most of the meal behind a large newspaper. Meanwhile, Mrs Fox drones on about how busy she is at work at the moment – she's a lawyer or something – while he just mutters things like "yes my sweet" and "you poor thing".

"You'd better be getting dressed now, Dylan," Mrs Fox says to me, eyeing the kitchen clock. "And please try not to be clumsy today. I don't want you ripping your school jumper again."

A vision of Tom grabbing hold of Dylan and ripping his jumper flashes before my eyes. I vaguely remember laughing when it happened.

Still feeling like the walking dead, I go back upstairs, get dressed in Dylan's clothes, then stumble out of the house. I'm fifty metres down the street before I realize I haven't a clue where I am or how I'm supposed to get to school.

Then I hear running footsteps behind me, and a breathless voice: "Hey, Dylan! Wait up!"

I turn around, and let out a groan. It's Andrew Crabtree, Dylan's equally geeky best mate, puffing and wheezing his way towards me.

"Get lost, moron," I scowl, thinking I'd sooner die than show up at school with a loser like him.

He stops in his tracks and frowns at me. "Dylan? What's wrong?"

"I'm not Dylan. Now scram, toe-rag, before I empty your rucksack all over the road."

After casting a final panicky glance at me, Andrew scuttles away.

I follow him at a safe distance and, sooner than expected, we turn a corner and there's the school.

In the playground, I go straight up to Dev and Tom, who are both sprawled on our usual bench. I know it'll be awkward at first, explaining my appearance, but it shouldn't take them long to realize I'm really their old mate Simon.

"Alright?" I grin at them. "How's my crew this morning?"

They both take one look at me and start laughing.

"Have you finally lost your mind, Foxy?" splutters Dev.

"You don't speak to us, doofus," warns Tom. "And I wouldn't be in *your* crew if you paid me! Now why don't you scuttle off back to geek's corner before Simon gets here – unless you want a flushie."

I picture pushing Dylan's head into the toilet while Tom flushes it – one of my favourite tortures. Of course, now that Dylan's head is *my* head, it doesn't seem quite so funny.

"Listen guys," I say calmly, "you've got this all wrong. I'm *Simon*. I may look like Dylan right now, but it won't last. Just a temporary malfunction in the appearance department – know what I mean!"

I start laughing, making like the whole thing's a big joke – but they don't join in. In fact I can tell they're running seriously short of patience.

Tom balls his hands into fists and gets to his feet, towering over me. Tom and I are usually the same height, but this morning I find my eyes are level with his chest.

I start to back off. "Wait!" I say – and then I play my trump card: "If I'm not Simon, then where is he? Huh? Why isn't he here?"

But this doesn't impress Dev and Tom as much as I'd hoped. In fact, they're barely listening. They just look past me, grins plastered across their faces. I turn to see what they're smiling at, and when I catch sight of it, I nearly fall over in shock.

Strolling across the playground towards us is... *me.*

I can feel my mouth try to form words, but my voice is trapped in my throat. What do I do now? I have to do something, but it's a struggle to breathe, let alone think. Who is that kid pretending to be me? How dare he? *I'm* Simon… aren't I?!

Suddenly Tom looms over me, shoving his ugly face into mine.

"Listen pipsqueak," he taunts, showering me with spittle, "if you want me to let you go before Simon gets hold of you, hand over your lunch money… NOW!"

I feel the anger rising inside me like a hot bubble. I'm about to shove him away, but as I raise my arms I realize that they're not my familiar muscular arms, but Dylan's puny ones. Even so, I'm not going to give in – I'd never do that! I can fight my way out of this… can't I?

Out of the corner of my eye, I spot Mr Grimes chatting to some students on the other side of the playground. If I shouted, he'd hear me… I'm sure of it. But that's the wimp's way out… not *my* way!

I should stand my ground, let the faker come over here, then I'll prove to him in front of everyone that there's only one Simon Archer…

Chapter 3

The Challenge

"C'mon, Foxy! Hand over your lunch money!" says Tom, grinning from ear to ear.

I narrow my eyes at him and puff out my puny chest. "Get stuffed!" I snarl.

Is that the first glimmer of respect I can see in Tom's face? My body may have changed, but I'm still as hard as nails inside, and he'd better get used to it!

"Have it your way then," he sneers and gives me a shove. I stumble backwards and collide with someone big and very muscular behind me. A burly arm spins me around, and there I am, face-to-face – or face-to-chest, to be exact – with the faker, the kid pretending to be me.

Up close, I was expecting to see some differences – you know, like different colour eyes or hair or something – but he's the absolute spit of how I used to look, even down to the scar on his cheek.

"What do *you* want, Foxy?" he growls. "Didn't you get enough punishment yesterday? Or did you enjoy it so much you've come back for more?" His hands are curling and uncurling, like mine always do when they're itching to punch someone.

"I'm not Foxy," I tell him, trying to stay calm – though I can't keep my eyes off those fists.

Behind me, Tom and Dev start laughing like a pair of asthmatic hyenas, but I keep going. "And you're not Simon," I tell him, "because *I* am, and there can only be one Simon Archer. Right?"

"You've lost it big time, Dylan," sniggers Dev.

My lookalike scowls at me, and I can't help feeling impressed – *did I really used to look that scary?* I can see he's dying to hurt me. His eyes flicker towards Mr Grimes. Luckily, the teacher's too close for him to risk anything now, but I know he'll come after me later. I know because that's exactly what I would do, and this other Simon seems to be like me in more ways than just looks. I have to act now – prove that he's a fake, before he gets his chance to make mincemeat of me.

I notice that a small crowd of kids has gathered. They've sensed that trouble is brewing. I'm pleased about this. They all know me, and they know my history in this school. If I quiz the faker on some of my legendary deeds, and he can't answer my questions, he'll be exposed in front of everybody for the fraud he is….

"Alright," I say to him, "if you're Simon, you should remember this one. What did I once do with the sugar in the staffroom?"

His frown deepens, and I start to smile. I've got him first time.

But then he says, "*I* swapped it for salt, obviously."

Okay, okay, maybe that was *too* famous. I should try and think of something a little more obscure.

"Who found a dead rat in her bag?"

"Cerys Jackson," he shoots back.

"What was her crime?"

"Not giving up her seat to me on the bus."

Huh! The faker is better than I expected.

Then I remember one of my most secret escapades. Only Tom and Dev ever knew about this one....

"Okay, tell me this," I say, "What did I once do to Ravi Khan?"

I wink at Tom and Dev, and I'm pleased to see their mouths fall open and their eyes widen with surprise.

For the first time the faker seems lost for words.

"You see," I say to everybody. "I've proved it. There's only one Simon Archer – and it ain't him!"

Suddenly, the faker grabs my collar in one of his brawny fists and lifts me clear off the ground. Now we really are face to face, and I'm close enough to feel his hot breath on my cheek as he says, slowly and menacingly, "How d'you know it was me who locked Ravi in the stationery cupboard?"

He throws me to the ground and snarls: "You're getting a double flushie for this, Foxy. Just you wait!"

The air is filled with giggles from all the kids watching us. Normally that's such a sweet sound, because it means I've made someone look stupid and won myself some laughter as a result. But right now it feels like needles in my ears.

They're laughing at *me!* They think *I'm* the idiot. They think *I'm* Dylan Fox.

Heat rises in my cheeks. I'm angry and embarrassed. I have to show them this isn't what I am. They have to understand that I'm the victim of a terrible mix-up. But first I need to win back some power and status in this school, I need to get back in with my old mates, even if it means – for now, at least – pretending to accept that Fake Simon is the real deal.

"Alright, lads," I say to Tom, Dev and the faker. "Just let me be part of your crew, okay? Let me prove myself. Set me a challenge. I'll do anything…."

I'm on my knees as I'm saying this and shamefully close to begging – but what choice do I have?

Unfortunately, my little speech only makes everyone laugh even louder. Tom is pounding his knees and sounding like a broken foghorn.

"*You!* In our crew?" he guffaws. "Get lost, loser!"

The school bell rings. I'm about to crawl away into a dark corner to lick my wounds, but then Fake Simon speaks up. "Tell you what, Foxy," he says. "If you can climb up on to the school roof at morning break, we'll think about it."

The school roof!

I look up. Tom and Dev are snorting their approval at this idea, clapping Fake Simon on the back for his brilliance. As far as they're concerned, this can only end in my total humiliation. After all, everyone knows that only one kid has ever successfully climbed on to the school roof – and that's Simon Archer!

They must think I'm madder than ever when I just smile and say: "No problem. You're on!"

* * *

Word quickly spreads through the school about what I'm planning to do, and by the time morning break rolls around, there's an even bigger crowd than before gathered in the playground by the boys' toilets – the favoured place for attempts on the school roof. At the front of the crowd, looking like a panel of ultra-mean *X Factor* judges, stand Fake Simon, Tom and Dev. They're grinning like demons at the prospect of watching me fail and most likely injure myself in the process.

As I squint up at the brick wall and the grey-tiled roof above it the school suddenly seems a lot taller than it used to be. I'm trying to remember how I climbed up last time when someone runs up and grabs my elbow.

It's Andrew Crabtree. "Hey, Dylan," he says hoarsely. "What's got into you this morning? Why are you doing this?"

I shrug him off, embarrassed to be seen with him. "Just lay off me, alright? You're not my mate, never have been."

Andrew backs away, disappointed. "You don't have to prove yourself to those idiots," he says. "You're better than this." Then he turns and pushes his way back through the crowd.

I move closer to the wall and place the fingertips of both hands in a couple of crevices where the cement has chipped away. *Yes, it's coming back to me now!* I heave myself upwards and find a tiny foothold where I remembered it, a couple of feet above the ground.

Using a nearby drainpipe for support, I lever myself upwards until my foot finds a crumbling window ledge. I grab the frame of the window and haul myself fully up on to the ledge. I'm now halfway there – further than most kids ever get. Glancing back over my shoulder, I get a quiet thrill from the worried look on Fake Simon's face. This wasn't what he expected or wanted.

A shy voice in the crowd suddenly shouts: "C'mon Dylan!" This is followed by a squeal as Dev reaches back and thumps my one and only supporter.

To my right, in line with my hip, is a long, shallow crack in the wall. If I can wedge my toes in there, I'll be able to grab hold of the gutter, then heave myself up on to the roof, just like I did before.

The toes of my right foot slot in easily, and by grabbing on to the top edge of the concrete frame above the window, I can get my left foot in beside it.

Nearly there now. Just one last big effort and my old crew will have to accept me back!

I look up… and gasp.

The gutter is a lot higher than I remembered.

Of course it is. I was Simon Archer last time I did this, not little Dylan Fox!

Even so, I can't turn back now, not in front of everyone. I have to try, at least.

I reach up and manage – *just!* – to curl my fingers around the gutter. Then I start to pull myself upwards. I pull and I pull, squeezing my eyes tight shut and straining my muscles to their limits. But it's no use. Dylan's arms are feeble!

I can feel my fingers start to slip. Desperately, I kick around, trying to find my old foothold, but I can't. My grip fails and suddenly I'm groping air. A second later, the hard playground flies up and smacks me in the face.

I lie there, trying to gather my thoughts.

What's happened to me? Am I really Simon Archer, or am I just going nuts? Who wakes up in someone else's body? I don't understand. I just want things to go back to normal.

Pain jolts through me as I try to move my arm and the left side of my face feels as if it's been sizzled in hot fat.

I want my mum!

Tom and Dev's laughter echoes around me like the braying and clucking of farm animals. But this is quickly drowned out by an even louder sound… the voice of Mr Grimes.

"What the devil is going on?" he thunders.

It's funny, that's the question I've been asking myself all morning.

I open my eyes.

The other kids, including Fake Simon, Tom and Dev, have all scarpered. Grimes reaches down with his one arm and helps me to my feet. Then he hands me a clean white handkerchief. I wipe some blood from my cheek and my legs immediately turn to jelly.

Come on body, man up a bit!

"I'm surprised at you, Dylan," Grimes says to me. "I never expected to see you trying to impress the likes of Simon Archer. You've got a bright future ahead of you…. Don't throw it away by getting in with *that* crowd. Now why don't you go to the medical room and get yourself cleaned up?" Dabbing my cheek with the hankie, I watch him walk away.

The likes of Simon Archer… that crowd…

He's talking as if 'Simon Archer' is some kind of disease to be avoided at all costs. Is that really what people think of me?

Chapter 4

Detention

The day doesn't get much better after that. The curse of looking like Dylan Fox continues, and I start to get the horrible feeling that I may have changed into him permanently. Either that or I really have gone totally crazy.

At the end of the school day, I head for the exit, planning to go home – my real home. Surely Mum, of all people, must be able to recognize her own son. But before I can leave the school building, I'm stopped by Mr Webb from the IT department.

"Dylan, I understand you attempted to climb on to the school roof today," he says, eyeing me reproachfully. "As punishment Mrs Hollins has set you an hour's detention after school."

"What?" I huff.

"She also nominated *me* to supervise this detention. So, as it is a first offence, I suggest you come along to computer club as usual and serve your sentence there."

I groan inside. The thought of having to mingle with all the geeks – kids I usually enjoy picking on – fills me with nausea. Reluctantly, I follow him into the lab.

At my workbench is the mangled robo-hand that I remember gleefully smashing under my heel yesterday.

"So unfortunate that it got run over by your dad's car," Webb mutters sympathetically.

Is that what Dylan told him?

"Still," he goes on, "I've no doubt a boy of your talents will have it fixed in no time."

After that, Webb goes off to help another kid, and I'm left staring at the crushed gizmo, wondering what I'm expected to do with it. I pick it up and put it down a few times, but don't make much more progress than that.

When Mr Webb returns twenty minutes later, his eyebrows shoot up almost higher than his head. "What's going on, Dylan?" he cries. "Why haven't you done any work on your project?"

"Maybe I can help," pipes up a voice behind us. I don't even need to turn around to know it's that Andrew Crabtree again.

Mr Webb just shrugs and leaves us to it.

Andrew turns out to be surprisingly friendly, considering how rotten I've been to him all day. Pretty soon, he's busy hammering, drilling, grinding and welding new bits of metal to replace the ones that were bent and twisted beyond repair. All the while he's talking away, cheerfully explaining to me what he's doing, and not minding a bit that I'm letting him do all the work.

As I watch him, I notice his left eye still bears the traces of bruising from that time a few weeks ago when I hit him for not handing over his lunch money. I really wish I hadn't done that now… or at least not punched him so hard.

* * *

At the end of computer club, Andrew asks me if I fancy coming back to his house to play video games. I mutter something about having other plans and make a quick exit. I feel this need to be by myself right now, to try and figure out what my next move should be.

I'm wandering past the sports hall when I hear some sort of commotion inside, so I poke my nose in to see what's going on. The hall's empty apart from Fake Simon, Tom, Dev and a girl who I recognize as Clare Philpott, the secret eater in our class. The three lads are picking on her, pushing her around. They laugh as she squeals at them to let her go.

Normally I can't stand misfits like Clare Philpott so it ought to give me a thrill to come across a sight like this, but surprisingly I don't feel that way right now. It's strange, I almost feel as if I should go over and help her. *What is happening to me?*

While I'm standing there, pondering what to do, Fake Simon suddenly looks at his watch and grunts: "Argh, I've forgotten I'm supposed to be somewhere. Gotta' go, fellas!"

I quickly scoot behind a pillar as he heads out of the hall and down the corridor. Now I'm suddenly curious about where this double of mine has to go to so urgently. Maybe if I follow him I'll find out who he is, and what's really going on.

Chapter 5

An Unexpected Meeting

"Leave me alone!" Clare cries. I look back and see that Dev and Tom have cornered Clare by the climbing bars. They're taunting her, calling her names. She's not looking at them, though. She's looking straight at me, pleading with her eyes for some help. I shrug, and mouth a *sorry* to her. I kind of mean it, too. The usual excitement when I see someone being pushed around just isn't there today. I almost feel as if I would help her if I could. But right now I've got more important things on my mind, like finding out where Fake Simon is off to in such a hurry.

I run after Simon down the corridor, keeping to the shadows and hoping he won't hear my footsteps. One of the advantages of being small, I'm discovering, is that you're practically invisible.

Fake Simon makes a sudden swerve to the right and heads through an exit into the playground. I follow him to a nearby bus stop, where he boards a double-decker bus into town. I manage to sneak on after him and we head down the high street. As we're approaching the town park, he presses the stop button. Hiding behind a group of people, I follow him off.

When I catch sight of him again, he's crossing the road. There's a man waiting there for him by the war memorial – a big man with broad shoulders and a shaved head. It takes me a moment to realize who it is, as he's the last person I expected to see.

Dad!

I haven't seen him for months! I'm about to run over there and give him a hug. Dad'll recognize me, for sure! He'll know what to do....

But then I stop, because (and this is really horrible) Fake Simon has just run up and hugged him. There's an awful, empty, burning feeling in my chest. Normally when I feel like this I want to punch someone, really hard, to remind myself how strong and hard I am. But right now I feel weak and useless, as if I don't even properly exist. Punching someone won't change that.

Dad's smiling and exchanging greetings with the faker. How can he possibly think he's his son? And what about me? Where does that leave me?

I watch as the two of them walk into the park and go and sit on a bench by the duck pond. I remember that pond from when I was younger and Dad was still at home. We used to go there as a family and feed the ducks. It's painful seeing the faker sitting there chatting and laughing, as if it's *his* dad he's with. It feels as if a stranger has come out of nowhere and trampled all over my life, my memories.

I want to run away before I do something stupid like going over there and thumping him. But on the other hand, I want to hear what they're talking about. Maybe – *hey, this is an interesting thought* – maybe that's not really Dad over there. Maybe that's, like *Fake* Dad, and Fake Dad and Fake Simon are behind this whole plot to take over my life. They're probably meeting now so that Fake Simon can update Fake Dad on how it's all going. If I could secretly listen in to what they're saying to each other, I could expose the whole thing.

Next to the bench where they're sitting is a big old willow tree, its branches thick with leaves that droop all the way to the ground. A perfect spot for a bit of eavesdropping.

The two of them are facing the pond, so they don't see me as I run across the grass behind them and push my way through the curtain of willow branches. I crouch down behind my leafy screen, not five metres from where they're sitting. Fake Simon is talking....

"Why can't I see you more often, Dad?"

"It's been difficult, son. You know me, always busy. But I'm here now, right?"

This isn't what I was expecting. So far, it sounds just like a conversation *I* would have with Dad. I so much wanted to believe otherwise, but I suppose I have to accept that it probably *is* my real Dad over there.

"So how's school?" asks Dad.

"Not bad." Fake Simon gives a little chuckle. "Had a weird day, though. There's this kid, Dylan Fox – 'Foxy', we call him. Anyway, today, he went a bit mad. He started telling everyone he was *me!*"

Hearing this, I flush red with anger and embarrassment. My fists clench, but I force myself to keep quiet and carry on listening.

"Probably just jealous, son. I'm sure a lot of people would like to be you."

"Huh! Yeah, too right. Anyway, this kid Foxy was so desperate to get in with me and my crew, he tried to climb up on to the school roof. Seriously! Of course he couldn't, and he fell flat on his face. Huh! What an idiot!"

Dad laughs. I'm surprised by the harshness of his laugh – it's like he doesn't even care that someone got hurt. Did he always laugh at my stories like that? Maybe I just never noticed before.

"Shows how much people look up to you, Si," Dad chortles. "The things they'll do to impress you! But you still rule that school, right, son?"

"Right, Dad."

"Just like I did, back in the day." He sniggers. "So how's your Mum? Still as useless as ever?"

Fake Simon laughs at this and says: "Yeah, pretty much." Usually I'd laugh with him, too. But strangely I don't like hearing Dad say that about Mum. I mean I know she drives me nuts at times, but at least she's been there for me – which is more than can be said of Dad. And compared to Dylan's mum, she's not so bad after all.

Crouching like this is making my legs ache. I shift a bit to try to get more comfortable, but this makes me lose my balance. I try to grab hold of a branch, but can't stop myself from falling to the ground in full view of Dad and Fake Simon.

"That's Foxy – that's the kid I was telling you about!" says Fake Simon.

"Well, well," says dad, advancing on me. "I hear you're my son's number one fan!" He smiles, but it doesn't look friendly somehow.

"Umm, well… I wouldn't really say–"

"The thing is, you'll never be as great as my son." He pulls Fake Simon into a headlock and ruffles his hair. "'Cos there's only one Simon Archer, ain't there lad."

"Yeah," mumbles Fake Simon as Dad releases his grip.

"Well–" I begin.

"Ooh, look out Dad," Fake Simon continues. "Foxy wants to hit you. Mind you, I doubt you'd actually feel it." They both crack up.

I turn and walk away, my teeth grinding with bitterness and frustration.

"I'll sort him out, Dad," Fake Simon shouts, heading after me.

"Nah son, leave him to sweat it out," grunts Dad. "Deal with him at school tomorrow!"

Chapter 6

More Surprises

I take the bus back to school, then retrace my steps to Dylan's house. Where else can I go, looking the way I do? I'm feeling hungry when I get in and I'm hoping there'll be some tea waiting for me. Dylan's mum is there in the kitchen, working on her laptop, but there's no sign of any food. She looks up as I come in.

"Where have you been?" she asks sternly.

"Er…."

"You should have been home an hour ago at least. And why is your cheek all black and blue?" She gives me a fierce frown. "Dylan, I don't know what's come over you lately. Do you have any idea how hard I've worked today, and how exhausted I am? The last thing I need when I come home is the sight of you looking as bruised as a peach. What on earth happened?"

I start to make up some story, but she quickly interrupts. "Stop! I really don't have time for this, Dylan. I'm on a tight deadline with this case, and now you're distracting me...."

As she's saying this, I get a flashback to a day last summer – I remember arriving home from the park with a black eye after I'd got hit by a cricket ball. Mum, my *real* Mum, was in the garden, hanging out the washing. When she saw me, she dropped the shirt she was holding and ran straight over, saying: "Oh, my poor dear. What happened to you? Quick, let me put an ice pack on that...." She'd cooked me my favourite tea that evening to help make me feel better.

I could really do with some of Mum's fuss and sympathy right now, but Dylan's mum clearly wants me out of her sight. "Just go and do your homework or something, will you?" she says, turning back to her laptop.

"I'm quite hungry," I tell her. "When's tea?"

She sighs. "Can't you see I'm busy Dylan? You know where everything is. Why don't you make yourself something?"

My blood heats up. *How can she not even give her own son food when he's hungry? What kind of a mother is she?*

I open a few cupboards looking for something to eat, slamming them shut as I go. Dylan's mum tuts once or twice, but doesn't comment. In the end, having found some bread and cheese, I make myself a sandwich and pour a glass of orange juice. Then I head for Dylan's room.

As I'm leaving the kitchen, I hear a strange noise coming from behind one of the doors leading off the hallway. It's a humming, beeping sound of high-tech machinery and seems out of place in a house. As I'm standing there, wondering what on earth I could be hearing, the door suddenly flies open to reveal Mr Fox. I'm so shocked, I nearly drop my orange juice. The humming noise is even louder with the door open and his face is lit by a weird greenish glow that's emanating from the room behind him. Mr Fox is staring at me so intensely it spooks me out. Before he can grab me and whisk me into his scary room, I dash up the stairs, into Dylan's bedroom and slam the door.

What was all that about?!

Maybe it's better not to know.

One thing's for sure, though: I so much preferred my old life. I'm starting to wonder how Dylan managed to cope with a mum who doesn't care about him, and a dad who's so, well, weird….

Speaking of Dylan, I wonder what's happened to him? I mean, if I'm in his body, then where's he? Maybe Dylan's the key to all this. Could he know what's going on – wherever *he* is? Perhaps I can find a clue somewhere around here. I scan the room. It's as dull as you'd expect for a room belonging to a nerd like Dylan: white walls; shelves crammed with books; that poster of the Periodic Table, and others showing Endangered Species of the World, a map of the Solar System.

I mean seriously! It's like being in a classroom. And none of it gives a hint about where he's got to and why I'm in his body. Then I notice the computer on his desk….

I go over and wake it up.

There's a half-finished geography assignment on there – which reminds me that Mr Grimes will be expecting that from me tomorrow. Well, too bad, Grimesy, I've got more important things to worry about right now. I start searching Dylan's hard drive for clues. I check his emails and his Instagram page. They're all normal, boring, day-to-day messages. It doesn't seem as if he had a clue he was about to disappear or be replaced.

I'm about to close down his computer when suddenly a message flashes up on the screen saying in huge letters:

SIMON ARCHER READ THIS!

I blink hard, but the message remains.

Woah, this is crazy! How does the computer know it's me?

Shocked, I click on the link beneath the message and a scan of a newspaper report appears.

Is this a clue about what's going on?

I start to read it....

HERO FIREFIGHTER RECEIVES MEDAL

A young firefighter was awarded the Queen's Gallantry Medal during a ceremony at Buckingham Palace yesterday. Part-time firefighter Tony Grimes climbed a ladder through smoke to rescue a woman and baby from a house fire. The woman, Janet Archer, and her infant son, Simon, were trapped in an upstairs room unable to escape. During the rescue, Mr Grimes sustained irreparable damage to his lower arm, which later had to be amputated...

The report goes on, but I can't read any more. I'm too shocked.

Grimes! I had no idea! And I thought my Dad was a hero. Where was he when we needed saving, when I nearly died?

I think about all the horrible things I've said to Grimes over the years. If only I'd known!

I wonder why he never told me the truth? He could have wiped that stupid grin off my face in a second. But he didn't.

I guess he didn't want to brag about what he'd done. Which is weird – I would have if I was him. For once I'm actually glad I'm Dylan Fox – at least he's always respected Grimes.

* * *

Next morning, I sit in the playground before school watching the other kids milling around in groups, chatting to each other. I don't want to see or speak to anyone. I'm too angry. I used to love school – loved the respect I got, the power I had over everyone. But I had to drag myself here this morning. I was really hoping that I'd wake up as myself, back in my old bed – but I didn't. I've had enough of this now. I don't know who I am or what's going on. I punch the wall beside me, feeling pain burn through my knuckles. I punch it again and again, but it doesn't help to clear my head.

What if I'm stuck like this for good? I need to sort myself out, make the best of it. But what kind of person should I be? Like my old self – or more like Dylan? I look at Dev and Tom play-fighting nearby. Should I keep trying to get in with them? On the other side of the playground Andrew is talking to a gaggle of geeks. He's been nice to me – maybe I should make friends with him.

But Dylan Fox is a nobody in this school. What's the point of being like him?

I grit my teeth. It's decision time....

Chapter 7

Loser!

I get to my feet and walk slowly across the playground towards Andrew. He's got his back to me, chatting with his geeky mates. "Hey," I say in my most gentle, friendly voice.

Andrew turns. His smile is a bit wary, as if he doesn't quite trust me. "Dylan. What's up?"

"Just thought I'd come over and say hello, y'know," I say to him.

He seems to relax then, and that's the moment I strike. I grab the strap of his rucksack and yank it off his shoulder.

Andrew's smile freezes and his eyes widen in shock.

It's vital that Fake Simon and my old mates see this next bit, so I shout out to them: "Hey,

Simon, Tom, Dev, look at this." Then I up-end Andrew's rucksack and start showering the playground with his books, pens and papers. Last to fall out is his plastic lunchbox. The lid opens as it hits the ground and his sandwich flops out, followed by his shiny red apple, which bounces and rolls across the tarmac to where Fake Simon is standing.

"See?" I say to them. "See what I did? I can join your crew now, right?"

The three of them just stand there and look at me, sneering. None of them says a word. A hush descends over the playground. It feels as if everyone has stopped what they're doing and is staring at me.

"I'm like you," I yell, staring right back at Fake Simon. "I'm hard, I'm tough, can't you see?" But as I'm saying this, my voice starts letting me down. It wavers, and I wonder how convincing I sound.

Fake Simon stoops and picks up the apple, rubbing it on his trouser leg. He walks over to Andrew and hands it back to him. Then he glances down at me as if I'm something nasty he's just stepped in.

I know that look – I used to practise it in the mirror!

"You're nothing like me, Foxy, and never will be," he says. "Once a loser, always a loser, and turning on your mates like that won't change anything. Besides, it ain't cool."

With that, the three of them turn their backs on me.

I slink away – from them, from Andrew, from everyone – wishing I could just disappear into a hole in the ground. I can't believe what an idiot I've been. I even made Fake Simon look nice by comparison!

Suddenly, the world seems a colder, darker place. The bell goes and we start to head in for our first lesson. I notice that no one wants to meet my eye. I'm alone and friendless, and it's all my own fault. Maybe Fake Simon's right. I'm nothing like my old crew now, and never will be. But where does that leave me? Where do I belong?

At lunch, I go and seek out Andrew. I find him in the library at one of the computer terminals.

"Hey, Andrew, I'm really sorry," I mumble.

He doesn't respond, doesn't even look up.

I offer him a fiver. "This is for your lunch." He doesn't take it, so I place it on the table next to him.

"Listen, Andrew," I continue nervously. "Do you, maybe, want to come round my place tonight? Play some video games?"

He bites his lip, but says nothing, just continues to stare at the computer screen.

So I leave him and make my way over to the lunch hall. Before I can get there, I'm ambushed by Clare Philpott. She's all tight-lipped and stiff-shouldered and I can tell at once she's cross.

"Why didn't you help me yesterday?" she says.

Huh! I'd almost forgotten about the sports hall incident in my long list of recent mess-ups!

I back away from her accusing stare. "You know there wasn't really anything I could have done. I mean those kids are a lot bigger than me."

"I didn't expect you to fight them off. But you could have gone and got a teacher."

I look down, a bit shame-faced. The thought of telling a teacher hadn't even crossed my mind.

"I don't know what's happening to you, Dylan." She continues. "You used to be… well, so nice, but now…"

"I'm sorry," I mumble. "Did – did they hurt you?"

"I'm ok," she says. "No thanks to you! It was just scary, the way they trapped me and wouldn't let me go. And they said some hurtful things. 'Greedy guts', 'guzzler', 'pig', things like that. But then what do they know?"

"You're right about them being scary," I say with a smile. "Simon and his mates are tough kids. They rule the school."

She frowns at me. "Do you really think that?"

I shrug. "Yeah, don't you?"

Clare shakes her head. "Maybe that's how they think of themselves, but I'm surprised to hear you say it, Dylan. Most of us just think they're pathetic."

"Pathetic?" How dare she?! My face heats up at this insult. Inside I'm still me – still Simon!

"Yeah, don't you feel sorry for them?" she asks. "The only way they can enjoy themselves is by hurting others. I mean how sad is that?"

"That's not the only way we–" I bite my tongue, remembering I'm supposed to be Dylan. But I can't believe that Clare Philpott of all people is calling us sad and pathetic. Clare Philpott, who's so greedy she has to have a second lunch halfway through the afternoon.

Then she brightens up. "So anyway, I've got permission from Mrs Hollins, Dylan. We're free to leave."

"Leave?" I ask, surprised. "What, leave school?"

She smiles and nods. "Just for the lunch hour. Remember, you said you'd give me a hand today?"

"Give you a hand with what?" I ask, but she's already halfway down the corridor.

"Come on, keep up," she calls.

Bemused, I chase after her.

We head out through the school gates and into the street. It feels strange but kind of fun being out of school at lunchtime, as if we're truants or something.

"Where are we going anyway?" I ask after we turn left into a street full of houses.

"Here," she says, pushing open a garden gate and walking up the path to a small bungalow. She opens the front door with a key, and calls out: "Hi Mum, it's me. I've brought Dylan with me, a friend from school."

"Hello, dear, come in," calls a frail voice from another room. "Come in, Dylan."

I follow Clare into the room where a pale, thin woman is lying in bed.

"How're you feeling, Mum?" Clare asks her. "You comfortable?"

"Back's hurting a bit, dear."

Clare starts adjusting the pillows to give her mum more support. "I can give you a back rub, if you like?" she offers. "And I'll make you some lunch."

I watch her fussing around her mum, and try to imagine my own mum if she ever became bedridden like this. How would I cope? Who would make my tea? And would I have to do the sort of stuff Clare's doing?

"Could you just help me to the toilet, dear?"

"Of course, Mum."

I shudder at the thought of having to do those things.

The lunch hour goes by, with Clare caring for her mum and me feeling mostly like a spare part. But, in the end, I do my bit to help, heating up some soup in a pan and serving it to Mrs Philpott with a couple of slices of buttered bread.

"Thank you so much, Dylan, dear," she beams as I hand it to her, which makes me feel unexpectedly warm inside.

"We'd better be getting back," says Clare with a glance at her watch. "See you soon, Mum."

We're about to leave when I remember that we haven't even had any lunch yet. When I remind Clare about this, she turns very apologetic. "I'm so sorry, I didn't think," she says. "Please, help yourself to a sandwich in the kitchen."

"What about you?" I ask her as I smear peanut butter between a couple of slices of bread.

"Oh, it's okay," she says patting her school bag, "I'll eat mine later."

That's when it hits me.

"You – you have to eat your sandwiches… in the afternoon, because… you spend every lunch hour caring for your mum."

"That's right," says Clare. "I thought you knew."

Now I feel terrible. "I'm sorry," I murmur.

"What for?" she laughs.

"For what I…. For the way Simon and his gang treat you."

"That's not your fault though, is it Dylan?" responds Clare as she ushers me out of her house.

* * *

That evening I'm sitting in Dylan's front room watching television when the doorbell goes. Mrs Fox is on the phone, deep in conversation about lawyer stuff, and to judge from the faint humming and beeping sounds I can hear, Mr Fox is busy in his scary room – so it's left to me to answer the door.

I'm surprised to see Andrew standing on the front step – so surprised I can't think what to say.

"Can I come in?" he says eventually.

"Sure," I say.

He walks in and heads straight upstairs and into Dylan's room, plonking himself down on the bed as if it's his own. Then he reaches over and starts checking out a magazine called *Robot News* by Dylan's bed.

"That was horrible what you did this morning," he says, still flipping through the pages of the magazine.

"I know," I say, sitting down on the desk chair and putting my head in my hands. "I'm pretty confused right now."

"What's got into you? Why are you trying to be friends with scumbag Archer?"

I'm about to make up some excuse for my behaviour, but then I decide I'm sick of all the pretence. So I tell him the truth: "I don't actually want to be friends with Simon – Fake Simon, as I call him – but what choice do I have? You see – he's me! Well, I'm him! I used to be Simon Archer."

Chapter 8

The Message

Andrew's face creases into a frown. "You what?"

I try to explain: "Two nights ago I went to bed in my house, as Simon, and the next morning I woke up in that bed you're sitting on, as Dylan Fox. I swear! This isn't my body. This isn't my house. And those two people downstairs are definitely not my parents."

He stifles a giggle. "You've really lost it, Dylan."

I sigh and scratch my head.

"Anyway, you told me all that mind swap theory was rubbish," he adds carelessly.

I look up sharply. "What?"

"You know, all that stuff you were talking about a few months ago, about scanning people's minds and transferring them into other bodies. You were totally obsessed, reading loads of books about it. Then all of a sudden you dropped it – said it couldn't possibly work."

When I hear this, my heart starts bumping like a Lamborghini doing a hundred miles an hour on a cobbled street. "Did Dylan, I mean *I*, ever show you any of these books I was reading?" I ask him.

Andrew shakes his head. "No, you were pretty secretive about the whole thing."

I turn in my seat and wake up Dylan's computer. Googling "mind swap" gets me nowhere, so I start on another search through his hard drive, looking for anything that might be related.

Andrew comes and peers over my shoulder. "You don't remember any of this then?"

"Of course not," I say through gritted teeth. "I'm not Dylan, am I? My mind's been swapped into his body, and now I've got to figure out a way of reversing the process."

"Are you being serious?" Andrew asks, and I nod, grimly. "Well then I suppose we could always check out their weird basement?" he suggests.

I swivel towards him. "The basement?"

"Yeah! I mean I know you're… or rather Dylan's… always telling me never to go down there, but maybe it's got something to do with all of this."

I remember the strange noises and lights and Dylan's dad coming through the basement door looking suspicious.

"Has Dylan told you anything about the basement – anything at all?"

"Not much. Only that your – I mean his – dad's a physicist or something and it's his personal laboratory. He conducts top-secret experiments down there – stuff he wouldn't dare try at the university where he works. I can't believe I'm having to explain all this to you – but I guess you're… you're not really you, are you."

"You think Mr Fox might have something to do with all this?"

"It would make sense, wouldn't it? I mean where else would Dylan get the equipment to carry out a… a mind swap."

I rise to my feet. "You're right. Come on, let's go down there now. I want to get this sorted."

Andrew shakes his head in wonder. "You really aren't like Dylan at all," he says. "He was always scared stiff of his Dad. Said he'd never set foot in that basement in a million years."

We're about to leave the room when a message flashes up on the screen. It's just as big and bold as the message I saw there yesterday. It reads:

SIMON ARCHER
KEEP OUT OF THE BASEMENT.
IT'S DANGEROUS!

Andrew nearly falls over in shock when he reads this. "Wh– Who sent that?" He looks around, scared, as if expecting to see someone crouched behind the wardrobe spying on us.

"How could they know we were thinking of doing that?" he whispers.

"Maybe it's Mr Fox," I whisper back. "He's probably got the house wired for sound. He obviously doesn't want us to go down there, which means he's got something to hide. Come on, let's go!"

"Wait!" says Andrew. "There's another message."

I look back at the screen. Now it reads:

SIMON, IT'S DYLAN
STAY AWAY FROM MY DAD
COME TO THE OLD ABANDONED
WAREHOUSE ON CANAL STREET

"Maybe we should go there instead," urges Andrew.

"But that's exactly what Mr Fox wants us to do," I fume impatiently. "Don't you see? He's sending us off on some wild goose chase to a warehouse, so he's got time to get rid of any evidence of this 'mind swap' experiment. If I don't go down to the basement right now and force him to reverse what he's done, I might be stuck as Dylan forever!"

"But what if Dylan really is trying to help you?" Andrew counters. "Maybe he wants his body back, too!"

Chapter 9

A Change of Mind

I'm itching to go down to the basement and confront Foxy's dad, but something about what Andrew just said holds me back: what if these messages really *are* from Dylan? He has to be somewhere, right? And he must want his body back as much as I want mine. Maybe the computer is the only way he can communicate now....

"Okay," I say to Andrew. "We'll do it your way. Let's go to the warehouse."

* * *

Canal Street is a dingy, run-down sort of place. Tom, Dev and I sometimes hang around here, though. We've broken into the warehouse a few times, but there's not a lot to see in there.

I wonder why Dylan – if it *was* Dylan – told us to come here.

I lead Andrew around the back of the building where I know there are a couple of loose boards on a window. It takes almost all of my puny Dylan strength to drag them away. Before I climb through, I glance back at Andrew. He's looking nervous. I can tell this isn't his kind of place.

"Coming?" I say.

"Okay," he shrugs, trying to look brave.

The inside is just as dark and grim as I remember from previous visits, with rusting pillars and big black oily puddles all over the concrete floor. Evening light streams through the smashed-in windows and broken roof tiles.

I don't exactly know what I expected – a high-tech lab, would have been nice, with some sort of headset I could put on with electrodes and stuff, and a button I could press to make me *me* again. Now *that* would have been cool. Anyway, I expected something better than this!

"We've been conned," I scowl. "There's nothing here. Let's go back to Dylan's place and raid that basement before it's too late!"

"Hang on," says Andrew. He's wandered over to one of the corners and is lighting up the graffiti-covered wall with the torch on his phone. I go and join him.

"What is it?" I ask, scanning the wall.

"Over there," he says, pointing.

I read the spray-painted writing. It says:

SIMON ARCHER LOOK HERE.

"It's another message from Dylan," says Andrew. "Look, there's an arrow underneath, pointing downwards."

We stare at the floor beneath the arrow. There's nothing there but a pile of old bricks. I start burrowing into it, shoving the bricks aside, hoping that there might be something useful hidden underneath. At the bottom of the pile I find a metal box.

I pick it up and force it open.

"It's empty!" I huff. "See, I told you – it's all just a waste of time."

"Maybe you're right," says Andrew grimly.

Angrily, I hurl the box to the ground.

"What do we do now?" muses Andrew.

Then, a voice behind us says: "Looking for this Foxy?"

We both whirl around.

A couple of boys are standing there. I recognize them from school. One of them, Brendan Harris, is dangling a thin little piece of white plastic between his fingers – a memory stick.

"Found it in that box," says Sadiq Hassan, the other boy.

"That must be what Dylan sent us here for," Andrew whispers.

"If you want it, it'll cost you," Harris taunts me.

The heat rises in my cheeks, and my fists start to clench and unclench. I want to wipe the smirk off that kid's face. But of course I know I don't stand a chance in Dylan's body. And I'm fairly sure that Andrew would be totally useless in a fight.

"Maybe you should offer them some money for it?" Andrew whispers to me.

But that's not how I do things.

Then an idea pops into my head.

"Nah, that's okay, you keep it," I say to the boys. "Come on, Andrew. Let's get out of here."

Andrew's staring at me. "Seriously?"

"Yeah," I say carelessly. "Of course Simon won't be too pleased when we tell him you've stolen his stuff, but that's *your* problem, not ours."

"Wait," says one of the boys, a little nervously now. "You're here for Simon?"

"That's right," I say, pointing at the name up on the wall. "That memory stick belongs to him and he sent us here to fetch it. But I'll just say that you two wouldn't give it to us. I'm sure he'll be very understanding. Right, Andrew?"

"Right," he grinned.

* * *

Minutes later we're on our way back to Dylan's with the memory stick safely in our possession.

"That was brilliant!" laughs Andrew. "A real brainwave. Just the sort of thing Dylan would have done, in fact!"

I frown at him. "I'm not Dylan, remember that! I was just… er… adapting a bit. If I'd had some muscle, I'd have shown those kids.…"

"Yeah, or you could have got yourself beaten up, and the memory stick might have been broken. You see, using your head, you got what you wanted and no one – and *nothing* – got hurt."

"Alright, alright!" I say impatiently. But I have to admit, he has a point.

Chapter 10

Answers

Back at the house, we sneak upstairs and plug the memory stick into Dylan's computer. Andrew's been buzzing with excitement about what we'll find on there, and I have to admit it's started to rub off on me. Perhaps I'll finally get the answers I've been looking for. He clicks on the icon when it appears and a video screen pops up, showing a freeze frame of Dylan's head and shoulders.

It's not what I expected.

In the background, I can see the wall of his bedroom – the room we're in now. According to the date in the top corner, the video was recorded three days ago – the day before I was transformed. Andrew presses play, and Dylan starts talking:

Hello Simon, he says, his eyes staring into mine almost as if he can actually see me. *If you're watching this, then Dad's experiment has gone wrong. I'm very sorry about that. He's a brilliant scientist, but sometimes he gets… well… sort of… carried away. You'll want to know what's going on, so I'd better start from the beginning. A few months ago, Dad invented a device for scanning people's minds and then copying them into another person's brain. So far he's conducted successful trials on rats and monkeys, but he wanted to see if the device would work on humans. He needed two subjects for the experiment. One of them is me… the other one is you.*

"Why me?" I rage at the screen.

Obviously I volunteered… and we chose you because you're… well, you've not been very nice to me. I thought it might do you good to see the world from the point of view of one of your victims.

"You little…" I try to reply, but Dylan is still talking.

I'm sorry about that. I realize you didn't have a choice in this. But then, if you think about it, you never bothered about my feelings, or Clare's or Andrew's or any of your other victims' either, did you?

Andrew glances at me as Dylan says this, but I don't meet his eyes.

Dylan continues: *I made Dad promise that the mind swap would last no more than a day. I didn't think it would be right for it to go on any longer than that. He gave me his word, but… to be honest I didn't completely trust him, which is why I set up that alert on my computer.*

I thump the desk in exasperation. "So you left me at the mercy of your nutter of a dad. Thank you very much, Dylan! If I was me again I'd–"

To stop the experiment, Dylan goes on, *and to transfer yourself back into your own body, you'll have to hack into Dad's computer. That means you'll need to log in remotely, using a password I will give you. Now listen carefully…*

I'm glad Andrew is here to follow Dylan's instructions, as they sound like total gobbledygook to me. Hunched over the keyboard, Andrew's fingers fly around the keys as new windows pop up and strange-looking programs are downloaded. Unfortunately, when Andrew tries keying in the password Dylan gives him, it doesn't work. He tries it three times with no success, then tries it three more times with slight variations. Eventually, he leans back with a frustrated sigh.

"Dylan's dad must have changed the password without telling him. Maybe he knew Dylan would try something like this."

Andrew has his hands in his hair as he's saying this, but on the screen, the cursor suddenly starts moving again, closing down windows and moving icons into the trash.

"What's going on?" I ask him.

He stares at the screen in alarm. "It's Mr Fox! He must know what we're up to." Andrew starts frenziedly typing. "He's gained remote access to this computer, but I think I can block him, if I can just...."

His hands are moving in a blur, and the screen has become a flickering battleground of opening and closing windows. Panic builds inside me. What chance does a schoolkid like Andrew have against a ruthless headcase like Mr Fox? It looks as if I'm doomed to stay in Dylan's body forever. Mr Fox may have told Dylan that the experiment would be temporary, but he obviously didn't plan on keeping his promise. He doesn't care about me or my life. As far as he's concerned, I'm just one of his lab rats.

Suddenly, Andrew gives a yell of triumph. "I'm in! Now I just need to follow Dylan's instructions…" He doesn't say anything else for a while. Finally after a lot more typing, he hits return, then looks at me.

"Dylan?" he asks.

"Nope," I reply. "It's still me!"

"Oh," says Andrew, his shoulders sagging. "Well, that's it. I've done everything that Dylan said. It should have worked…."

* * *

"It should have worked…"
"It should have worked…"
"It should have worked…"

Andrew's words are still echoing in my brain as I open my eyes.

I'm in my bed. My ACTUAL bed! In my ACTUAL bedroom! And it's morning.

I leap out and run to the bathroom. Staring back at me from the mirror is… *me*. Simon Archer! The handsome hunk is back!

A massive grin splits my face and I start laughing and singing and dancing around the bathroom. Then I run downstairs and hug Mum. "It's me!" I tell her. "I'm back!"

She stares at me, baffled. "Back from where, dear?"

"Never mind," I smile. "It's good to see you. And hey, you look… well… you look nice today."

Mum seems shocked and smiles back uncertainly. "Thank you, Simon. It's very… um… *nice*… of you to say so! Are you feeling alright?"

On the walk to school, I can't help singing. I even jump up and punch the air a few times. People stare at me but I don't care. When I get to the playground Tom and Dev are lounging on our usual bench, I swagger up to them, full of the joys of spring. "Morning, lads."

"Morning, Simon," they chorus.

No hesitation. They recognize me!

"You look pretty chuffed," chortles Tom. "What've you been up to then, Mr Archer? Chucked Cerys Jackson in the pond again or something?"

"C'mon, let's have all the details," says Dev, drawing closer.

I shake my head. "Nope. Just feeling, I don't know… happy?"

Mr Grimes wanders by, and I call out to him, "Morning, sir."

He stops and glares at me suspiciously, wondering if I'm mocking him. "Morning, Simon," he replies, sounding a little confused.

Shortly after this, Dylan and Andrew enter the playground.

"Oh, look, there's our mate Foxy," chuckles Tom.

"Shall we give him a flushie?" cackles Dev.

"Nah," I say, and I nod towards a grassy area where some kids are kicking a ball around. "I can't be bothered with all that any more. Let's go and play some footie instead."

Tom and Dev head off to join the game, but I linger, waiting for Dylan and Andrew to pass by. When Dylan sees me, a brief smile flickers on his face.

I smile back, then run off to join my mates.

THE END

FICTION EXPRESS

THE READERS TAKE CONTROL!

Have you ever wanted to change the course of a plot, change a character's destiny, tell an author what to write next?

Well, now you can!

'Mind Swap' was originally written for the award-winning interactive e-book website Fiction Express.

Fiction Express e-books are published in gripping weekly episodes. At the end of each episode, readers are given voting options to decide where the plot goes next. They vote online and the winning vote is then conveyed to the author who writes the next episode, in real time, according to the readers' most popular choice.

www.fictionexpress.co.uk

WINNER
Education Resources
Award for Innovation

FICTION EXPRESS

TALK TO THE AUTHORS

The Fiction Express website features a blog where readers can interact with the authors while they are writing. An exciting and unique opportunity!

FANTASTIC TEACHER RESOURCES

Each weekly Fiction Express episode comes with a PDF of teacher resources packed with ideas to extend the text.

"The teaching resources are fab and easily fill a whole week of literacy lessons!"
Rachel Humphries, teacher at Westacre Middle School

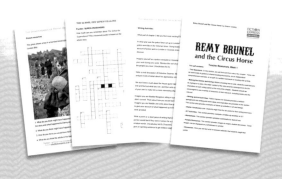

Have you read *The School for Supervillains* yet? Here is a taster for you…

Chapter 1

Welcome to St Luthor's

Mandrake DeVille sat in the back seat of her parents' armoured limo as it wound up the mountainside. A sheer drop fell away to the car's left. To the right rose a mossy cliff-face.

The bulletproof window reflected her face back to her: black eyebrows, naturally slanted into a scowl, a small, mean mouth, and a long, pointy nose. Her black hair hung over one eye in a sinister curtain.

It was an evil face. Mandrake wound down her window so she didn't have to look at it.

Far below lay a valley of dark trees, and she caught the faint scent of pine. On top of a distant mountain peak, she could see an ancient castle, with turrets and high, black stone battlements.

A loud BLIP BLEEP came from the car's GPS. Mandrake leaned forwards. "What's that?" she asked the chauffeur, sharply. "Are we close to St Luthor's?"

St Luthor's School for Supervillains was Mandrake's new school. She was looking forward to her first term there about as much as a mouse looks forward to being ripped into mincemeat by a cat.

"I'm not sure what's going on," said the chauffeur, peering closer at the screen. He yanked on the steering wheel, but it didn't move. A note of panic entered his voice. "It's… I think someone's taken control of the car!"

What? Mandrake wondered. *My parents have excellent security. How could someone hack–?*

But then she stopped wondering.

She was too busy screaming.

The car was speeding off the edge of a cliff towards the wooded valley floor far, far below.

* * *

Mandrake knew in one part of her brain that they were plummeting downwards but time seemed to pause, hanging in the moment they soared off the cliff. Images flashed behind her eyes.

Then, a memory of her mother earlier that morning. Duessa DeVille was dressed for work in her Doctor Death costume, with its skull mask, long black cloak and spike-heeled boots.

"Just remember," she had said, as Mandrake climbed into the limo. "I checked your DNA carefully before growing you in the lab. One day, you could be as great a villain as I am. Who knows, maybe your telekinetic powers might even rival my own.

"Which means," her mother had continued, pointing a finger cruelly, "any failure will be entirely *your* own fault. So, do NOT let me down. Stay strong and, more importantly, stay alive. I'd be shamed in front of my fellow villains if any child of mine showed weakness. And if you were to die… well, I'd be utterly humiliated."

Mandrake had nodded and rolled her eyes. She'd heard this all before. She knew her mother didn't actually love her enough to care if she died. And her father, Torquemada, hadn't even bothered to say goodbye. Not surprising, given that his favourite catchphrase was '*Supervillainy begins at home*'. And what's more villainous than neglecting your daughter?

Or, as both her parents preferred to call her, their 'spawn'.

Right now, Torquemada DeVille – a.k.a. Stormfront – was off threatening some Pacific island or other with extinction if its government didn't hand over their royal jewels. He wasn't bluffing. His power over storms, typhoons and other dangerous types of weather was legendary. He could easily unleash a tidal wave huge enough to flood a small country, as long as most of it wasn't too far above sea level.

Her parents expected her to become just like them. Evil. A supervillain. A master criminal. An enemy to superheroes everywhere.

But, in spite of all their efforts, she was *nothing* like them.

I'm not evil, Mandrake thought. It was a truth she barely dared to acknowledge at home, in case her parents' psychic security minions were close enough to read her thoughts.

But now, falling to almost certain death, she thought it loud and unafraid: *I don't want to be a supervillain! I want to be a superhero! I want to save the world from people… like my parents. But I'll never* be *anything unless I pull it together.*

Mandrake's mind suddenly cleared. She felt incredibly alert. More awake than she had in years.

Pull yourself together. Or you'll be a smear on the valley floor.

Mandrake closed her eyes and focused, just the way her powers tutor had taught her. She reached deep inside, allowing her power to come to the surface.

If she could just slow the car down, even a little, perhaps she could survive this?

She heard the wind rushing past the window, the chauffeur's desperate howl. It was no good. She couldn't keep her focus. She wasn't trained, not properly. She was barely able to lift an orange, never mind stop a two-tonne car in mid-air.

I'm going to die.

She watched as the ground rushed to meet her. Perhaps the car would explode? *At least it'll be a dramatic exit.*

* * *

Except, all of a sudden, the car was no longer falling. In fact, there was no longer a car.

Mandrake was standing on solid ground, in the dark. Her skin tingled, as though she'd had a mild electric shock. She felt utterly lost. It was so dark that little specks of light danced in front of her eyeballs like fireflies.

Where am I? What happened?

Mandrake held out her hands, meeting nothing at first, then her fingers brushed against skin. She flinched, and the skin's owner gasped.

The skin felt cold and unnaturally smooth to the touch. *Who has skin like that? Or what?*

Suddenly the lights came on. She was in a large, ancient hall with wood panels and a high, vaulted ceiling.

I'm inside St Luthor's. They must have teleported us. Skin-tingling was one of the side effects of teleportation. She knew this from years of family holidays. Mostly to warzones and the sites of horrific disasters… many of which her parents had caused.

She looked around.

Is this the castle I saw in the distance?

There was a group of about thirty teenagers with her in the hall. All of them seemed as scared and confused as she felt. They were mostly superhumans, but there was the odd alien too – including one *very* odd alien. He was green-skinned with eyes on stalks, standing close beside her. She realized it must have been him she'd touched in the dark, and looked away in embarrassment.

She turned her gaze to the long table at one end of the hall, where a row of terrifying figures sat looking at them with disdain.

Those must be the teachers.

The staff at St Luthor's were all retired supervillains. They wore robes, in many rich patterns and a rainbow of villainous shades, from gold and green to black and red. Their faces were the stuff of nightmares. Some were scarred, some simply monstrous, others were stunningly beautiful but so cruel you could barely look at them. Every one of them had a glint of pure, true, unmistakable evil in their eyes.

Suddenly the old man at the centre of the table rose to his feet. He wore green robes with a high, sharp collar. His eyes were green, too. He had probably been handsome, once upon a time. But now he must be ninety years old. A scar slashed his wrinkled face into two distinct parts.

"Welcome," he said, in a low, silky voice. He slid his hands behind his back and linked them there. His eyes flicked to Mandrake for a moment, and his scar-split lips curled into a smile. It was horrible. Then his gaze flicked away. "I am the headmaster of this academy. You may call me," the smile widened and grew crueller. "Master."

Mandrake wished he'd stop smiling.

FICTION EXPRESS

The School for Supervillains
by Louie Stowell

Mandrake DeVille is heading to St Luthor's School for Supervillains, where a single act of kindness lands you in the detention pit, and only lying, cheating bullies get top marks. On paper, Mandrake's a model student: her parents are billionaire supervillains, and she has superpowers. The trouble is, Mandrake secretly wants to save the world, not destroy it.

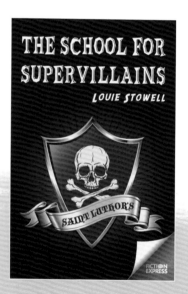

ISBN 978-1-783-22460-9

FICTION EXPRESS

Drama Club
by Marie-Louise Jensen

A group of friends are involved in their local youth drama club at a small city theatre. When their leader, the charismatic Mr Beaven, announces he wants to put on a major new play at the end of the summer holidays, the cast is very excited. Amidst rivalry, hopes and disappointments, will there be more drama on or off the stage? And who will get the leading roles?

ISBN 978-1-783-22445-6

About the Author

Alex Woolf was born in London in 1964. He played drums in a teen band, and, in his 20s, he rode his motorbike and travelled in America (where he nearly ended up as a barracuda's lunch!). In between, he did lots of dull and dangerous jobs. His worst job was washing up in a restaurant kitchen full of cockroaches!

Finally, he settled down to write books. Alex has written non-fiction books on subjects like sharks, robots and the Black Death, but his greatest love is writing fiction, and he claims to have been writing stories almost since he was able to hold a pen.

His other books for Fiction Express include the 'Time Detectives' series in which Joe and Maya travel back in time to solve mysteries. He has also written *Chronosphere*, a science fiction trilogy about a world in which time moves super-slow, and *Aldo Moon and the Ghost of Gravewood Hall*, a story about a teenage Victorian detective who investigates ghosts in a spooky old mansion.